To Winter:
Always carry at least one lantern.

Special Thanks:
Special thanks to Integrity First Limousines, FLOW, SPAA, Ragdale, Kelvin Johnson and Vaunasha Mosley-Boyd. We will be forever grateful for the ways you supported and encouraged the birth of this book. You are the best!

Copyright 2016 First Flight Publishing Co.

Author: Lucille U. Freeman
Photography: Alaina Johnson, Chiam Johnson, Kashshawn Johnson, Lucille U. Freeman
Set Design: The Johnson Family
Actors: Mikayla Johnson, Jadyn Johnson, Ethan Johnson
Book Design & Layout: Rosemarie Gillen
Editor: Janet Cheatham Bell
Project Manager: Kashshawn Johnson

ISBN-13: 978-1945596001
ISBN-10: 1945596007


First Flight Publishing Company
P.O. Box 2166
Matteson, IL 60443-5166

Printed in the U.S.A.

First
Flight
Publishing Co.

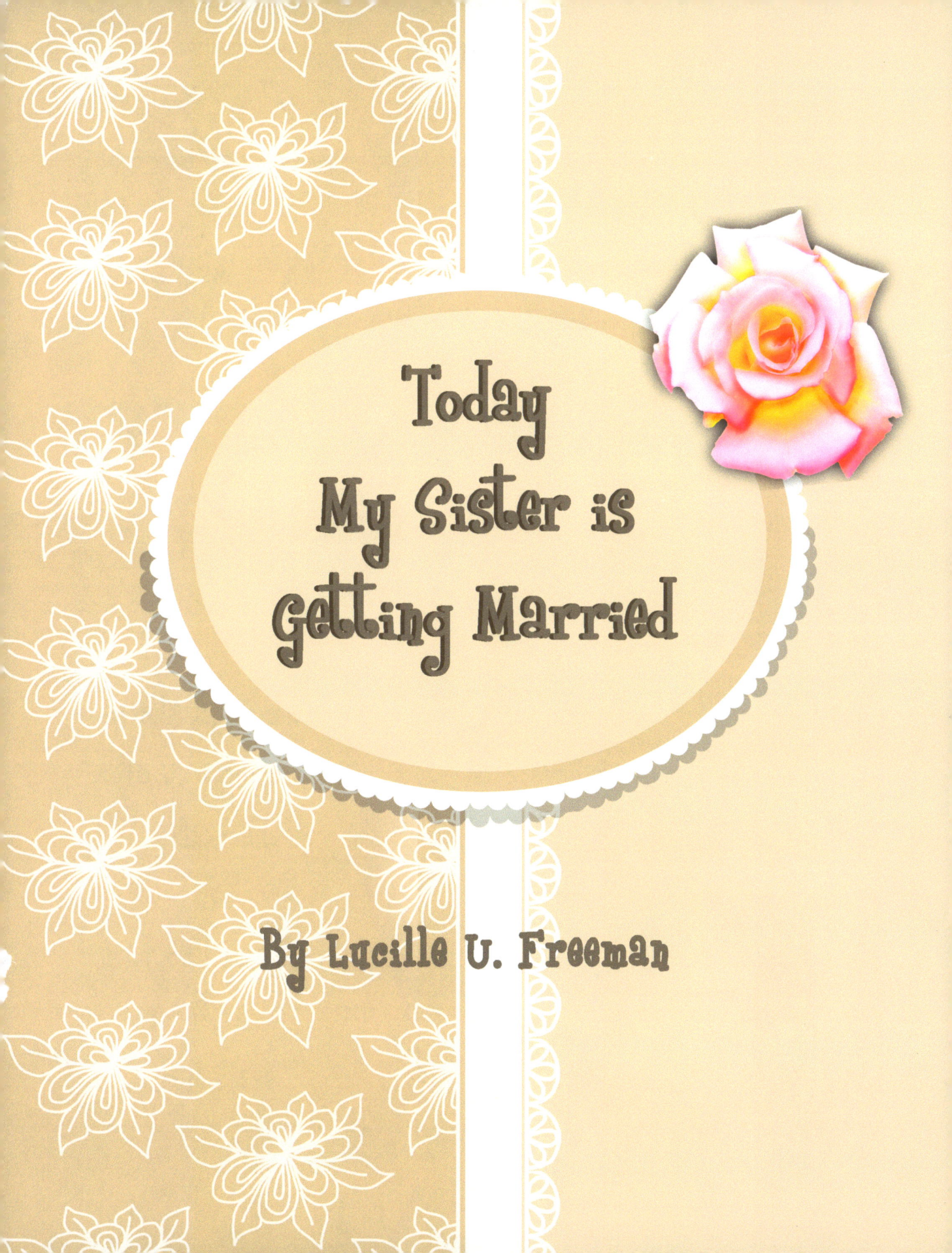

# Today
# My Sister is
# Getting Married

### By Lucille U. Freeman

Today my sister is getting married.

Mom says she is moving out of the house...

But not too far away, I can visit her.

We've shopped for her dress
and shoes to match.

Mom and Dad bought
her a wedding cake.

They made a list
and sent
out invitations.

Today
my sister

is getting
married.

The minister is ready.
A limousine is waiting outside
our house.

After the wedding there's going
to be a big party.

Mom calls the party a reception.

She says there will be music and dancing.

Everyone will be all dressed up for my sister's special day, including me.

I have a big job to do, Mom says.

I have to put
flowers on
the path so
my sister can
walk
down the aisle
to start her new
life...

Today my sister is
getting married.

Mom says I am the
flower girl and
I'll do a good job.
I will...

...because I
want my

sister to
be happy!

Mom says we will dress our best for my sister's special day.

All of our family will be there to celebrate with us.

My sister's best friends will be wearing matching dresses and carrying flowers. Mom says they will be called bride's maids.

I asked her how could maids clean in those dresses; and besides everything looked pretty clean already. Mom only smiled.

Today my sister is getting married.

The music has started. Mom and Dad are sitting on the front row. David will be her new husband, Mom and Dad's new son, and my new brother.

Today my sister is getting married. I see our neighbors and friends. There's grandpa and grandma, my uncles, aunts and cousins.

Everyone is quiet for a minute, then my song begins... They all stand when I walk down the aisle. I want to laugh and cry, I'm not sure why... I decide to be brave and smile.

# Coming in September 2016

# SILLY CATERPILLAR

No one knows the potential inside of you.
A story about being your best in spite of criticism.